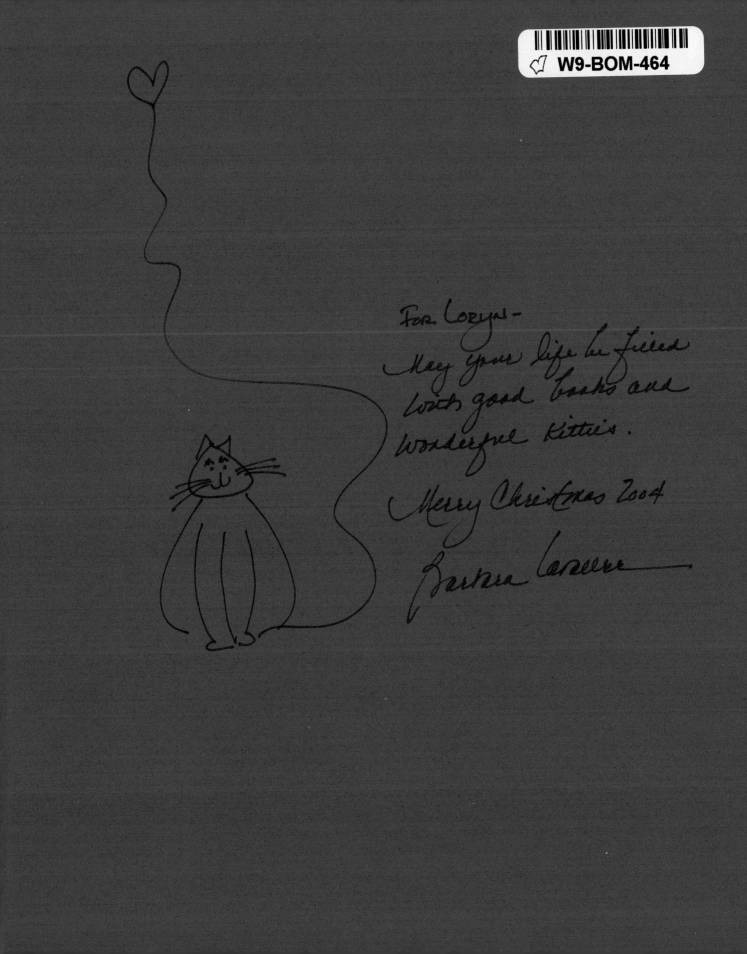

W9-BOM-464

For Loryn —

May your life be filled with good books and wonderful kitties.

Merry Christmas 2004

Barbara Cancere

Groucho's Eyebrows

Written by Tricia Brown

Illustrated by Barbara Lavallee

Alaska Northwest Books®

Kristie stamped the snow off her boots and burst in the front door. Frosty air swirled in around her. Ever since she'd stepped off the bus, she had been wanting a hot mug of cocoa with marshmallows. But she forgot all about it when she saw what her mother was holding.

"O-o-o-o-h, Mom! Is he ours? Does he have a name? Can I hold him?" The questions came tumbling out.

As Kristie ran her hand over the kitty's back, he arched against her warm touch and seemed to smile.

"Yes, he's ours," her mother said. "Well, yours, really. And no, I don't know his name. But those funny eyebrows remind me of a famous man who made people laugh.

"Let's call him **Groucho.**"

To Kristie, Groucho's eyebrows looked like
nature had made a mistake. She covered them
with her thumbs and looked at his face.

"Where'd you get those goofy eyebrows, hmmm?"
she said sweetly. "You'd look better without them."

Still, she grew to love Groucho more every day.
She liked to dress him up (he didn't mind) and
carry him everywhere. Groucho hung around
Kristie's neck like a little monkey.

"That cat's going to forget how to walk!"
her mother laughed.

Groucho

CAT
TALES

And Groucho liked to watch Kristie get ready for school. He'd nest on her still-warm pillow as she put on layers of clothes—tights, pants, shirt, sweater, snowsuit, clunky boots, hood, scarf, and mittens.

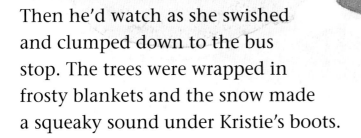

Then he'd watch as she swished
and clumped down to the bus
stop. The trees were wrapped in
frosty blankets and the snow made
a squeaky sound under Kristie's boots.

When she looked back, Kristie could see Groucho pawing
at the window, sad that his favorite girl had to go to school.

On sunny days, they'd go
outside for a special game
of hide-and-seek. Groucho
got to be *Nanook* (an Eskimo
word for polar bear), and Kristie
was the great Arctic tracker.

As she stalked around the cabin with her imaginary
spear, Kristie always pretended not to see Groucho.
But he couldn't hide those black eyebrows in the snow.

"I found you again! I win!" she would cry, sweeping
the cat into her arms. "You're so easy to find with
those silly eyebrows, Groucho-boy."

Every night, Groucho would paw softly at Kristie's shoulder until she'd lift the covers and let him curl up next to her. Together they'd snuggle under the thick quilt, keeping out the chilly air.

Kristie once saw a kitty that had stayed out too long on a wintry night. His once-pointy ears were now round nubs, like a bear cub's. Kristie shuddered whenever she thought about it. She'd rub Groucho's furry ears and whisper,

"Don't worry, I'll take care of you."

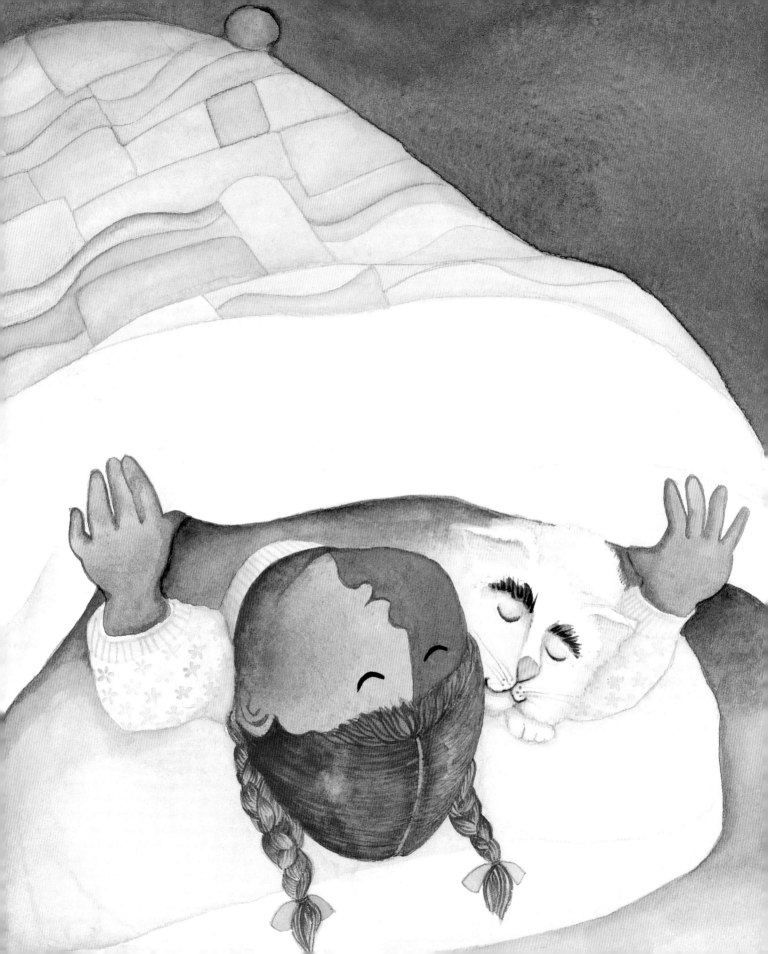

One day, a deliveryman brought a package for Kristie's mother. As she signed the papers, Groucho slipped outside to find Kristie for a game of Nanook. He forgot that she was still at school.

When Kristie came home, Groucho wasn't at the door to greet her. She looked everywhere for him. On the couch. Under the quilt. Behind the woodstove.

He was gone.

"GROU-cho! Grouchagrouchagroucha GROU-cho!" she called from the porch, hoping he'd come running in like he always did. But he didn't, and Kristie's heart sank—it was getting dark out and starting to snow.

By bedtime, Kristie was worn out. She and her mom had knocked on every door in town asking if anyone had seen a white kitty with funny black eyebrows. But no one had seen Groucho.

"Tomorrow's a school day," her mother finally said sadly. "Time for bed."

But Kristie couldn't sleep. She couldn't stop the pictures in her head.

*W*hat if Groucho found a fox den
and the mama fox jumped out and bit him?

*Or, what if he ran into a porcupine and got quills
stuck in his nose and I wasn't there to get them out?*

Oh no! What if he scared a big old moose and the moose kicked him?

Kristie pulled the covers over her head as tears ran down her
cheeks. All she wanted was to snuggle with her best friend again.

At breakfast, Kristie didn't feel like eating. She didn't feel like going to school either . . . not today or *ever* again.

"I'm sure he's okay, honey," her mother said. "It didn't get very cold last night, even though we got some fresh snow."

Suddenly, Kristie had an idea. "I gotta go, Mom!" she hollered, and ran out the door.

Outside, Kristie
imagined herself as the
great Nanook tracker.
She spotted a line of
dainty paw prints
and thought,
*They're small,
but they might be his.*

Excited, she followed the trail.

But Kristie's heart fell when she saw a fox ducking into her den.

"I'm not giving up yet,
Groucho!" she grumbled to herself.

In a while, she spied another set of tracks.
These were set wider in the snow and had a broad smudge
between them. *Maybe Groucho's dragging something*, Kristie thought.
Maybe his leg? Could he be hurt?!

This time she ran up the trail.

Kristie didn't have to go far to discover
what was making those strange tracks. It was
just a fat porcupine sweeping the snow with his tail.

She sighed with relief, *Well, at least Groucho isn't hurt.*

Minutes later, she noticed yet
another trail veering off to one
side. The tracks were deep and
spread far apart from each other.
That could be Groucho's trail, she
thought, *if he were running and
jumping . . . maybe he's being
chased by a hawk!*

Off she went again, running as
fast as her boots would carry her.

At the edge of a clearing, Kristie stopped
to catch her breath and look for more signs.
She saw willow branches chewed off at the
same height, a pile of small, woody nuggets,
and a wide oval in the snow where a very
large creature had spent the night.

Uh-oh!

Moose!

Kristie's heart began to race.
I'd better get out of here, and now!

Kristie flew back down the trail. She dodged trees. She jumped over rocks. The woods were a blur. And yet, even at that speed, her keen eyes spied black spots on the white snow ahead.

Kristie's brain shouted *STOP!* and her feet obeyed even before she could think, *Hey, what's that?* It all happened so fast that she fell face first into the snow! And when she looked up, sure enough, there were two silly black eyebrows peeking back at her, like coal on a snowman's face.

"Groucho!

My Groucho-kitty!"
she cried happily.

Groucho yawned and blinked
lazily, as if to say, "That was the
longest game of Nanook we've
ever played. *Now* can we eat?"

Kristie banged
open the front door, yelling,
"Groucho's home! Groucho's home!"

Her mother hugged them both, then wiped away worried tears while she
made cocoa (and a saucer of warm milk for Groucho). As they nestled on
the couch, Kristie grinned at her favorite cat in the whole world and said,

"You know, maybe those silly eyebrows aren't so silly after all.
I never would have found Groucho without them."

"Well then, where is my black marker?" said her mother with a smile,
"I'd better put some on you, too, in case I ever have to search for my little
Nanook girl again!"

Dedicated with love to Kristen and Groucho, best friends forever.
—T. B.

To my cats, Nerm and Moonie,
who are my friends and models and frequent
leavers of footprints on paintings.
—B. L.

Groucho was a real kitty, eyebrows and all,
who was adopted by a little girl named Kristen.
They lived in Fairbanks, Alaska. One year Kristen entered
Groucho in a cat show and won a blue ribbon and a
silver trophy cup for "Most Unique Cat."

[PHOTO COURTESY TRICIA BROWN]

Text © 2003 by Tricia Brown
Illustrations © 2003 by Barbara Lavallee
Book compilation © 2003 by Alaska Northwest Books®
An imprint of Graphic Arts Center Publishing Company
P.O. Box 10306, Portland, Oregon 97296-0306
503-226-2402; www.gacpc.com

All rights reserved. No part of this book may be reproduced or transmitted in any form
or by any means, electronic or mechanical, including photocopying, recording, or by any
information storage and retrieval system, without written permission of the publisher.

Library of Congress Cataloging-in-Publication Data
Brown, Tricia.
Groucho's eyebrows / by Tricia Brown ; illustrations by Barbara Lavallee.
    p. cm.
    Summary: Even though she makes fun of his silly eyebrows, Kristie loves her cat,
Groucho, so when he disappears on a snowy night in the wilds of Alaska she worries
about everything that could happen to him.
    ISBN 0-88240-556-X
    [1. Cats—Fiction. 2. Lost and found possessions—Fiction. 3. Alaska—Fiction.]
I. Lavallee, Barbara, ill. II. Title

PZ7.B8185Gr 2003
[E]—dc21   2003045198

President: Charles M. Hopkins
Associate Publisher: Douglas A. Pfeiffer
Editorial Staff: Timothy W. Frew, Jean Andrews, Kathy Howard, Jean Bond-Slaughter
Production Staff: Richard L. Owsiany, Susan Dupere
Editor: Michelle McCann
Designer: Elizabeth Watson

Printed in China